have horse riding lessons

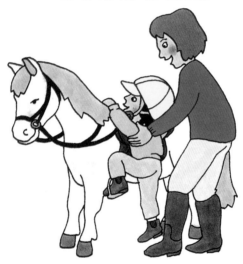

Jean and Gareth Adamson

Blackie Children's Books

BLACKIE CHILDREN'S BOOKS

Published by the Penguin Group
Penguin Books Ltd, 27 Wrights Lane, London W8 5TZ, England
Penguin Books USA Inc., 375 Hudson Street, New York, NY 10014, USA
Penguin Books Australia Ltd, Ringwood, Victoria, Australia
Penguin Books Canada Ltd, 10 Alcorn Avenue, Toronto, Ontario, Canada M4V 3B2
Penguin Books (NZ) Ltd, 182-190 Wairau Road, Auckland 10, New Zealand

Penguin Books Ltd, Registered Offices: Harmondsworth, Middlesex, England

First published 1989 by Blackie Children's Books
This edition first published 1993
5 7 9 10 8 6 4

Copyright © 1989 by Jean and Gareth Adamson

The moral right of the author and illustrator has been asserted

Made and printed in Great Britain by William Clowes Limited, Beccles and London

A CIP catalogue record for this book is available from the British Library

ISBN   0 216 92601 7 Hbk
ISBN   0 216 92600 9 Pbk

When Topsy and Tim went to watch
the Pony Club Gymkhana, they had a big
surprise. One of the riders was their
friend Josie Miller.

'Well done, Josie,' said Dad.
'Where did you learn to ride
like that?'
'At Mrs Reed's Riding School,'
said Josie.

Mrs Reed was at the Gymkhana too.
Mummy went to talk to her.
'Are Topsy and Tim old enough to have
riding lessons?' asked Mummy.

'What do you think, Topsy and Tim?'
said Mrs Reed. 'Would you like
to have riding lessons?'
'Yes, please,' said Topsy and Tim.
'I have a beginners' class every
Thursday,' Mrs Reed told Mummy.
'Topsy and Tim are the right age for that.
They can start next Thursday.'

'They must wear hard hats, in case of accidents,' said Mrs Reed. 'They should also wear proper riding boots. You can get everything at shops that sell riding things, new and used.'
'Will their wellies do?' asked Mummy.
'No,' said Mrs Reed. 'Wellingtons are too loose and can fall off.'

'Just one more thing,' said Mrs Reed.
'I hope you know your left from your right.'
Topsy and Tim wondered why.

'Do you know your left and right?'
asked Dad on the way back to the car.
'This is my left,' said Topsy.
'That's right,' said Dad.
'And this is my right,' said Tim.
'No,' said Dad. 'That's wrong.'

It was a long wait until their first riding
lesson but at last Thursday came.
Mrs Reed took Topsy and Tim to the
stables to meet their ponies.
Topsy's pony was called George.
A big girl called Julie was there
to look after George and Topsy.

Tim's pony was called Gipsy. Sally
was there to look after Gipsy and Tim.
Gipsy nibbled at Tim's hair. 'Stop it,
Gipsy,' said Sally. 'That's hair, not hay.'

Topsy and Tim led George and Gipsy
into the big riding school. It wasn't like
Topsy and Tim's Primary School. It was
an enormous barn, with soft, dry earth
on the floor.

There were some more children there,
already on their ponies.

Julie helped Topsy to mount George.
They stood at George's left side.
'First put your left foot up into
the stirrup,' said Julie.
'What would happen if I put my right
foot up first?' asked Topsy.
'You'd end up sitting back to front,'
laughed Julie.

'This is my left foot,' said Tim.
'Well done,' said Sally, as she helped
him to mount Gipsy.
It was nice being up on the ponies.
Sally and Julie stood beside them
and showed them the proper way
to hold the reins.

Mrs Reed explained to Topsy and Tim
how to start their ponies with a squeeze
from their legs, how to use the reins
to guide the ponies and how to stop them
by gently pulling on the reins.

Tim gave Gipsy a squeeze with his legs,
but nothing happened.
'Squeeze a bit harder,' said Sally.
Tim gave a bonk with both legs and
Gipsy started walking.
'That's right, Tim,' said Mrs Reed.

'Now use your legs to make your pony trot,' said Mrs Reed.
The ponies began to trot quite fast.
Topsy and Tim were bounced up and down on their saddles.
'Ow! Ow! Ow!' said Topsy.

They had to learn to rise up and down
in their stirrups to miss the bumps.
'You are doing well,' said Mrs Reed.
'I don't think Topsy and Tim are
beginners, they're doing so well!'

Topsy and Tim pulled their reins to stop their ponies. Now they had to balance without stirrups. Then they put their hands on their heads and shut their eyes...

'Now reach right forward to touch
your ponies' heads . . . and right back to
touch their tails,' said Mrs Reed.
It was fun!

Their first riding lesson was over.
Topsy and Tim dismounted.
'My legs feel all wibbly-wobbly,' said Tim.
'So do mine,' said Topsy.

They took the ponies back to their stables and helped to take off their saddles and bridles.

Tim patted Gipsy's mane and Topsy
hugged George.
'Thank you, ponies,' said Topsy and Tim.
'See you next week.'

First published in the uk, by R. K. Nixon Books in 2023

CW01020917

With special thanks to Emily x

For her love of dinosaurs and her help with the story.

Other books by R. K. Nixon

Nani & Friends:

The Prince Alexander Adventures:

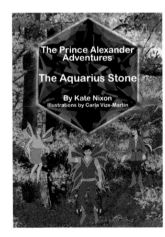

Visit www.rknixonbooks.com to order your next book.

My sister has a dinosaur that she keeps in the basement, but you can't keep a dinosaur in the basement!

He has ten blue spots and four green paws, white spikes on his back and big sharp claws.

He **ROARS** all day and **ROARS** all night and likes to give passersby a *FRIGHT*.

My sister has a dinosaur that she keeps in the basement, but you can't keep a dinosaur in the basement!

Every day he grows some more, his head sticks out of the window and his tail pokes out of the door.

My sister has a dinosaur that she keeps in the basement, but you can't keep a dinosaur in the basement!

She feeds him chocolate, biscuits and cake. He eats till he's sick and has terrible *TUMMY ACHE*.

My sister has a dinosaur that she keeps in the basement, but you can't keep a dinosaur in the basement!

He likes to drink tea from a blue china cup and makes loud *slurps* when he takes a sup.

My sister has a dinosaur that she keeps in the basement, but you can't keep a dinosaur in the basement!

When he poops he fills lots of carts but even worse is when he *farts*!

My sister has a dinosaur that she keeps in the basement, but you can't keep a dinosaur in the basement!

When he sleeps he snores so **LOUD**, birds fly away and animals hide underground.

My sister has a dinosaur that she keeps in the basement, but you can't keep a dinosaur in the basement!

He likes to sing and dance and shout. The whole house **shakes** when he jumps about.

My sister has a dinosaur that she keeps in the basement, but you can't keep a dinosaur in the basement!

When it rains he likes to **splash** his feet, sending tidal waves straight down the street.

My sister has a dinosaur that she keeps in the basement, but you can't keep a dinosaur in the basement!

He likes to have hugs and lots of cuddles but gets tied in knots and all in a muddle.

My sister has a dinosaur that she keeps in the basement, but you can't keep a dinosaur in the basement!

We love our dinosaur and we'll never be apart, and he loves us with his great big heart.

My sister has a dinosaur that she keeps in the basement, and you CAN keep a dinosaur in the basement!